Bunny Day

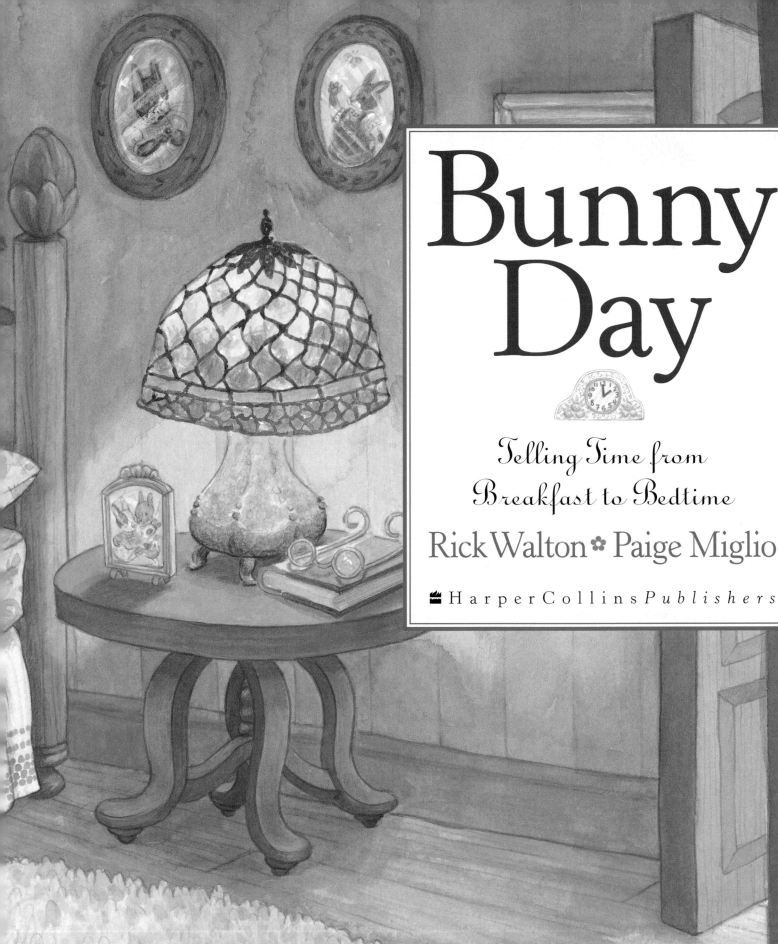

Bunny Day

Telling Time from
Breakfast to Bedtime

Rick Walton ❧ Paige Miglio

HarperCollinsPublishers

To April, David, Annika, and John Peterson,
on whose farm the bunnies were born
—R.W.

For Chris
—P.M.

"Bunnies, it is getting late!"
Father Rabbit says at eight.
"Time for breakfast, bunnies dear.
The sun is up and morning's here."

Faces washed until they shine,
Bunnies dress themselves at nine,
Brush their teeth, and do their chores,
Making beds and sweeping floors.

Brooms are put away, and then,
Bunnies go outside at ten
To help their father plant some seeds,
Water flowers, pull up weeds.

Bunnies bustle, and, thank heaven,
All is tidy by eleven.
Chores need doing every day,
But now the bunnies get to play.

Bunnies will be hungry soon.

Picnic's spread at twelve—that's noon.

Fruit and sandwich taste so good.

"Who would like some more?" "I would!"

"Ready, set? Now bunnies run!"
Mother Rabbit says at one.
"Race and chase and bounce a bit.
That will keep my bunnies fit."

A little rest is good for you.
It's time for bunny naps at two.
All around the house we see
Bunnies resting peacefully.

"Who will take a walk with me?"
    Mother Rabbit says at three.
Lots of little bunny feet
    Go out the door and down the street.

Pull the paper from the drawer,
Artists go to work at four.
Pens and crayons, scissors, tape—
Bunny art is taking shape.

Hungry bunnies all arrive
  In the dining room at five,
Set the table, take a seat,
  Put their napkins on, and eat.

Every bunny quickly picks
   One last game to play at six:
Hide-and-seek or steal the flag,
   Jacks or marbles, swings or tag.

Bunnies think that books are heaven.
Story time begins at seven.
One book, two books, three books, four.
"Please, please, Father, read some more!"

"Bunnies, it is getting late,"
   Mother Rabbit says at eight.
"Into bed. Turn off the light.
   Sleep well, bunnies dear. Good night!"

Bunny Day
Text copyright © 2002 by Rick Walton   Illustrations copyright © 2002 by Paige Miglio
Printed in the U.S.A. All rights reserved.   www.harperchildrens.com

Library of Congress Cataloging-in-Publication Data   Walton, Rick.   Bunny day / by Rick Walton; illustrated by Paige Miglio.   p.   cm.
Summary: A bunny family spends the day together.   ISBN 0-06-029183-4   ISBN 0-06-029184-2 (lib. bdg.)   [1. Rabbits   Fiction.   2. Family life   Fiction.
3. Day Fiction.   4. Stories in rhyme.]   I. Miglio, Paige, ill.   II. Title.   PZ8.3.W199 Bu 2002   00-054061   CIP   AC   [E] dc21

1 2 3 4 5 6 7 8 9 10 ❖ First Edition